Olga's Oggies

by Anne Adeney
illustrated by Leighton Noyes

Contents

PEARSON
Longman

This is dedicated, with much love, to my eldest daughter, Jenny – to remind
her of her childhood home in Plymouth.

1 In the Jungle

"These old bits of fence will make a great ramp once I nail them together," muttered Olga to herself. "Then I'll see how far I can jump! Now where did I leave my rollerblades?"

"Olga! What are those marks in the hall?" came a screech from the top of the stairs. Olga's mother looked with horror at the trail, which ran from the front door, across the hall to the bottom of the stairs, and then into the kitchen. The marks were small, even and bright, fluorescent green. She came rushing downstairs to investigate further.

Olga looked up from rummaging through the tool drawer in the kitchen. She'd found the hammer and was searching for some nails.

"Olga! What *have* you been doing? It looks like green paint! Aarrgh!"

There was a loud crash as Olga's mother's feet met Olga's rollerblades at the bottom of the stairs.

The house was ominously quiet, as both Olga and her mother remained silent for a moment in shock. Then came a ferocious roar.

"Olga!"

Olga dropped the hammer as if it was red hot. She ran through the kitchen door and down the garden path, her green footprints getting fainter and fainter as the paint was transferred to the path.

"I was making you a beautiful mural, actually," Olga muttered under her breath, as she sped along the path. Her class had made one in school last week and Mr Reilly had said it looked wonderful. It had, too. Their green, yellow, red and orange footprints had made trees and bushes as a background for their mural about autumn.

At school they'd all washed their feet in plastic washing-up bowls from the resources room, but unfortunately, today Olga had forgotten that bit. She'd left her mural drying in the garden, gone straight indoors to get her rollerblades, then suddenly remembered the old fence panels she had been saving to make something interesting.

There was a second crash as Olga's mother tripped over the hammer, abandoned on the kitchen floor. This sent Olga diving head first into the bushes. The far end of Olga's garden was dense and overgrown. Her dad took pride in his smooth lawn, his cherished rose bushes and his neat vegetable garden. But he had left a large area behind the greenhouse and the garden shed to the birds, the bees and the butterflies. It was mostly a dense area of tangled bushes and small, stunted trees.

Olga crawled into the bushes as far as she could. She came to a small clearing at the base of a little old tree, and sat with her back against the trunk. She pondered on the unfairness of life. All she'd been trying to do was to make her mother an interesting picture. It would have been perfect to put on the dining room wall, where last week

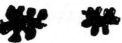

her chocolate yoghurt had exploded as Olga struggled to get the top off. The new wallpaper had soaked up the chocolate like blotting paper, and rubbing it had only made it worse.

Surely the paint should have worn off her feet by the time she got indoors. You'd think a sensible person would look where they were going, wouldn't you? Fancy Mum falling over the rollerblades! After all, the bottom of the stairs was a perfectly logical place to leave them, when you were going to sit on the bottom step to put them on.

Olga ran her fingers along the tree trunk behind her. The tree was covered in lichen, soft and springy like her father's beard, only grey-green. Olga giggled suddenly at the thought of her dad with a green beard. Then, in her mind's eye, she saw him as he would probably look soon, when Olga's mum told him about her exploits this morning. His face would go pink, then red, then purple. Steam would come out of his ears and flames from his mouth – or something like that.

"Perhaps I'll stay here a little longer," mused Olga, "until the first explosions have died down." But the good thing about her father was that once he had erupted, like the volcano Olga had seen on TV, he was fairly quiet.

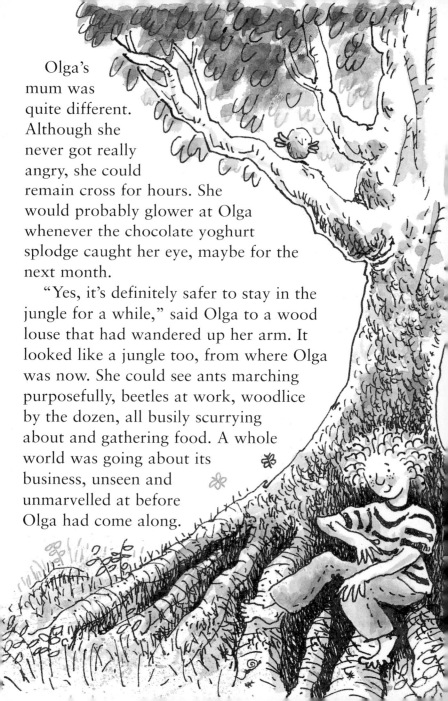

Olga's mum was quite different. Although she never got really angry, she could remain cross for hours. She would probably glower at Olga whenever the chocolate yoghurt splodge caught her eye, maybe for the next month.

"Yes, it's definitely safer to stay in the jungle for a while," said Olga to a wood louse that had wandered up her arm. It looked like a jungle too, from where Olga was now. She could see ants marching purposefully, beetles at work, woodlice by the dozen, all busily scurrying about and gathering food. A whole world was going about its business, unseen and unmarvelled at before Olga had come along.

There was just room for Olga to crawl a little further into the jungle. On hands and knees she crawled, slithered and pushed her way forward. She felt like an explorer, discovering the far distant parts of the world. Suddenly the dry, scrunchy leaf litter beneath her hands gave way and Olga fell, down and down into a deep, dark hole.

Olga turned over and over in a series of forward rolls that Miss Eagle would have been proud of if she'd managed them in gym class. As she fell, the image of Alice in Wonderland came to mind. Miss Eagle was reading it to them in class. Alice had fallen down a hole like this at the beginning of the story.

"But Alice fell asleep and dreamed it all," thought Olga. "I'm definitely wide-awake. I'm exploring uncharted territory." She loved new words, and racked her brain for a phrase Alice had used. As she tumbled down she seemed to be going slower and slower, instead of faster and faster. The words came to her as she landed gently on a pile of crackly leaves and dry moss.

"Curiouser and curiouser," thought Olga.

2 The Mine

Olga sat up and looked around her, shaking her tangled red curls off her face. Light filtered down from the hole above, and although she couldn't see the top of the hole, she could see her surroundings quite clearly. She got up from the nest of leaves. There was a tunnel stretching off into the distance. She looked up.

"If I was Alice I would find a little cake that says 'Eat me!'," said Olga aloud. "Then I could take a bite and grow tall enough to get out of this hole!" When Olga was a bit frightened she found that it helped if she said her thoughts aloud, as if she was talking to her best friend, Sam. She never wanted to look scared in front of him, so acting as if he was there immediately gave her courage. But there was no Sam and no cake and Olga couldn't climb back up again, so she set off down the tunnel.

Although the tunnel was long and twisting, it was light enough to see. The rocky walls seemed to be giving off an eerie light. She trundled along for what seemed like ages. She stopped at the end of the tunnel, suddenly frightened to go any farther. Perhaps she was in the sewer, or in the waterworks somewhere. Olga's knowledge of how the city worked was a bit vague, but she knew some of it was underground. Or perhaps they were making a tunnel from Plymouth, under the River Tamar to Cornwall, because there was always such a queue for the ferry.

She imagined an army of tall, bearded men like her father, just around the corner. They would all accuse her of trespassing, before turning pink, then red, then purple. Steam would come hissing out of their ears, and flames from their mouths … But Olga's curiosity was stronger than her fear. She could just see herself on the *West Country News at Six* – 'Fearless Plymouth schoolgirl discovers secret plans for Tamar Tunnel.'

That would be her introduction. Perhaps she'd get the afternoon off school to go to the TV studios, like her friend Katy had done when her mum and dad won a big prize for the toys they made. Olga would really enjoy being famous.

So she crept along the tunnel and emerged into

an enormous, brightly-lit cavern. The sight that
met her eyes made Olga's mouth drop open in
amazement. There were huge vats like giant
mixing bowls. Enormous machines that looked
like concrete mixers lay idle in the centre of the
cave. It all looked like some sort of factory.

On the right-hand side, Olga could see a gaping hole that was the entrance to another tunnel. Coming out of this tunnel into the main cavern were narrow railway tracks with empty, wheeled trucks on them.

Everything was coated with a thick layer of dust. Even the floor seemed to be ankle-deep in it. Looking back, Olga could clearly see the trail of her own footprints leading back into the tunnel. Obviously nobody had been here in a very long time.

Olga moved around a giant mixer machine. With a sigh of relief she noticed a gleam of light coming from a third tunnel on the far side of the cavern. There was no way she was going to explore the dark tunnel. She had been down a tin mine once, on a school trip, and the gloomy entrance looked just like that. She walked gingerly across the stony floor of the cavern. The dust cushioned her bare feet, but she was uncertain about what lay under the dust.

As she came around a huge vat, she suddenly stopped dead in surprise. There, set on a carved stone platform, was a small object. Perhaps it was treasure – a small chest full of jewels or money! Full of curiosity, she tiptoed over for a closer look. Wrapped neatly in brown paper, it looked just like someone's lunch. Olga giggled at the thought. The giggle echoed eerily around the dusty cavern, getting louder and louder. Without stopping to think, Olga grabbed the package and ran. She raced in the direction of the bright entrance and straight along the tunnel.

Olga ran and ran, the small parcel clutched tightly to her chest. Suddenly, almost without realising it, she burst out of the tunnel, and was outdoors again in the bright sunlight. She sank, panting, to her knees. It was a relief to feel cool grass on her bare skin again. She looked around in surprise. She knew exactly where she was.

It was a
small
park near
her own
home.
The park
gates were
just at the
end of her
road.

A huge oak
tree spread its
shady branches
overhead. The tunnel must have come out
from among the roots of the tree. Olga
scrambled around, looking for the hole she
had so recently come through. She must mark
the spot. She would come back with Sam and
explore the cavern properly, this time with
torches for the dark tunnel.

Guiltily, Olga looked down at the little
package she still held tightly in her hand.
She didn't know why she'd
taken it. The sound of
her own giggle had
frightened her
and she had

just
grabbed
it and
run.
"I'll put
it back,"
she told
herself
firmly, "but
not now, not
alone."

But search as she might,
Olga couldn't find the entrance
anywhere. She discovered what might
have been a rabbit's burrow, but that
was the only hole to be seen, and it was
tiny. She certainly hadn't come out from
there.

Puzzled and perplexed, Olga sank down on
the grass for a rest. She was still out of breath
from all that running and searching. She must
have been around the tree a dozen times.
And she was *dying* to find
out what was in the parcel.
Turning it over in her
hands before unwrapping
it, Olga was even more

convinced that it was someone's lunch. It was soft, and the paper was greasy. She hardly dared open it. Judging from the undisturbed dust around it, the tiny package must have been there for years, maybe even hundreds of years. But what if it was jewels? A diamond necklace hidden inside a sandwich perhaps. With fumbling, eager fingers, Olga unwrapped the package.

It was a Cornish pasty. A brown, semi-circular pastry parcel full of delicious meat and potato. In Devon, where Olga lived, they called them 'oggies'. A real Devon pasty was a tiddy oggie.

Olga was disappointed. She loved pasties – they were one of her favourite foods. But she had been hoping for treasure. Still, it looked like a particularly fine oggie. The pastry crust was golden brown, and it looked plump and delicious.

It lay on the brown paper, looking freshly baked, not years and years old. It looked good enough to eat. And what was that? Olga was suddenly enveloped by a luscious, succulent smell. She picked up the oggie in amazement, and immediately dropped it. The oggie was hot, as if it had just been taken from the oven!

A little plume of steam rose enticingly from the pasty and a gentle breeze sent the steam spiralling upwards. Then, the brown paper wrapping caught Olga's eye as it started to flutter away. She leaped up and grabbed it. She smoothed out the paper, her eyes searching eagerly for any clues it might hold.

As the sun shone onto the wrinkled, creased paper, black writing began to appear. Olga and Sam often sent each other secret messages written in lemon juice. It was invisible on white paper, but if you held it up against a heat source, like a radiator, the writing appeared, as if by magic. Now, the heat of the Sun was revealing a secret message. The writing was spiky and faint, but Olga just managed to decipher it.

Beware all ye who trespass on my domain
Don't seek to profit from unlawful gain.
Wondrous Oggies have the power
all men desire
Abuse that power, and your fate
will be dire.
If to any man the secret of the mine you tell,
You will surely break the power of
the Oggies' spell.
But if you keep the secret, ever hold it true
Every week an Oggie will appear for you.

An oggie mine – so that was where all the tunnels led! The cavern must have been some sort of factory. Olga struggled to make sense of the writing. It was both a threat and a promise.

Someone obviously thought their oggies were rather special. Was '**wondrous**' the same as wonderful … or something more? She knew '**dire**' meant 'something awful', but what would her '**fate**' be if she told the secret? And how could an oggie have a spell?

Olga shook her head. She didn't believe in magic! But what on earth was it all about? And since when did oggies come from mines anyway?

She wished Sam hadn't had to go and stay with his great-granny this weekend. Olga admired Sam's great-granny almost as much as he did. She always told them lots of stories, and some of them were seriously scary. Sam's great-granny certainly believed in magic! If *only* Olga could tell Sam about it. But that would probably break the spell and she didn't even know what the spell *was* yet!

3 Uncle Billy's Balloons

"Roll up, roll up! Come and see the fantastic
Uncle Billy and his balloons. He will amaze you.
He will astound you. He will astonish
you – and all for only a pound!"
Olga looked up in confusion,
then she remembered. Of
course! It was the day of the
Green Fair in Hawkins Park.
There would be jugglers and
acrobats, puppeteers and morris
dancers, and lots of other
entertainment. In the distance
Olga could see lots of bright-
coloured bunting where stands
had been set up. They would be
selling crafts and herbal
remedies, goat's cheese
and jewellery, toys

and crystals. It was always fun at the Green Fair and Mum had promised to take her that very afternoon. But that was before the incident this morning with the green paint.

Olga scowled in the direction of Uncle Billy. He was a fat, grumpy man who dressed up as a clown, did a bit of simple juggling, made a poor attempt at magic tricks, and made animals and things out of bendy modelling balloons.

She knew him from the last Summer Fayre at school. She'd stood beside him for ages, watching him twist and turn the skinny balloons into models. She'd only wanted to learn how it was done. Olga loved making things, and this looked like fun. He'd yelled at her. "Get out of it! Clear off, kid, and get your mum. I don't do this for free!"

But Olga had stood there, just out of reach, until she had learned to twist and turn lots of different models. Her father had bought her some modelling balloons for her birthday, and she'd made her own models since then. Uncle Billy charged a pound for a balloon model it took him only seconds to make. Olga knew that even the best modelling balloons cost only five pence each – what a rip-off!

Olga picked up the oggie again. It certainly looked good, and it smelled absolutely delicious.

Did she dare take a bite? Could it *really* be that old? She saw Uncle Billy take a pound from a little boy of about three. Olga saw him turn round and wave happily to his mum a little way away.

"He's making me a doggy!" he yelled at her.

Uncle Billy gave the dog's tail a last twist and set it down on the grass near the little boy. He hated children, and never actually touched them if he could avoid it. Before the child could even reach out for it a little gust of wind lifted the model and blew it a few feet away. It landed on some rough grass and burst with a loud bang.

The little boy howled and turned to Uncle Billy. "Want another doggy!" he wailed.

"Run along to your mum then, kid, and fetch another pound," said Uncle Billy, and started juggling.

Olga was absolutely furious. What a horrible man! Without thinking, she took a huge bite out of the warm oggie in her hand. She saw Uncle Billy's juggling balls fall to the ground.

Uncle Billy himself just stood there, his froggy eyes still looking at the place where the highest ball had been. His podgy hands were suspended in mid air, one high, one low.

The little boy was frozen, too, his arms outstretched, half-way towards his mum. His yelling mouth was wide open, but no sound came from it. Everywhere Olga looked see, people were suspended, motionless. Olga ran from person to person, her mouth still full of oggie. She couldn't believe it. What was happening? She went back to Uncle Billy. She noticed his nasty scowl on his red, painted-on mouth.

Olga swallowed her piece of oggie. Immediately Uncle Billy bent down to pick up his juggling balls, swearing loudly. The little boy started running again, and howling. Music played, people chattered, morris dancers danced. Amazed, Olga took another bite. Everyone she could see in the park was silent and motionless once more. So this was the wondrous secret power of the oggie. *Time stood still!*

Olga could hardly believe it, but already knew what wanted to do. Uncle Billy had already blown up about a dozen balloons. They were in a big tub behind him, all ready for modelling. Happily, Olga got to work. First, she made a headband with a feather at the back, and a sword with a curved handle like a cutlass.

Then she made a yellow bee with big orange

wings, a white swan, a purple kangaroo and a coiled-up snake. She even managed to get the snake's head to curve out like a cobra's. You had to suck the balloon in just the right place to do that. She twisted the green balloon into a funny bobbly caterpillar, and made a droopy flower out of the last few balloons. If the little boy didn't like it he could always give it to his mum. It was his mum's pound, after all.

Taking small rapid bites of the oggie, Olga drew faces, feathery lines and stripes on the balloons with Uncle Billy's wide black marker pen. Then, satisfied at last, she ran over to the little boy. He was still frozen in the middle of his frantic run back to his mum. She put the headband on his head and threaded his hand through the loops of half the models. She put the rest on his other arm and the sword in his hand. They certainly couldn't blow away now. Olga stood back to admire her work. That was more like a pound's worth!

Walking back to Uncle Billy, Olga was struck again by his ugly scowl and his bulging froggy eyes. He was trying to hide his real personality behind his happy, painted-on clown's face.

"What a cheat!" said Olga, aloud.

Taking Uncle Billy's own red spotted handkerchief, she reached up and rubbed away his face paint. She took the black marker pen and gave him a new face, following the natural lines of his own face. It looked good – nasty, mean and bad-tempered, just like he really was.

"People will think twice about giving you a pound now!" said Olga, with great satisfaction. She put the pen carefully back into his pocket.

The last bit of oggie in her mouth had melted down to almost nothing now. Olga quickly looked round for the grease-spotted piece of brown parchment. It had vanished as completely as the entrance to the tunnel. As the last of the oggie disappeared down her throat, Olga heard a ferocious roar from Uncle Billy. It almost drowned out the squeal of delight from the little boy. Olga took to her heels and ran home as fast as her dusty bare feet could carry her.

4 The Loophole

"What's going on, Olga?" asked Sam, running after her as she turned into her road after school on Monday. "You've hardly spoken to me all day! I'm sorry I had to go and sleep over at my great-gran's instead of going to the Green Fair with you at the weekend. But my mum *made* me go!"

"Oh, Sam, I'm not mad at you!" said Olga quickly. "I didn't even go to the fair. It's just … I can't tell … it's amazing … it's so awful … oh, Sam!"

"*What's* so awful, so amazing – so *secret* that you can't tell me about it?" he asked. "I thought we were best friends!"

"That's the whole point!" said Olga desperately. "It's a secret and if I tell, the spell will be broken!"

"A spell?" asked Sam, his big brown eyes lighting up with excitement. "Magic – like in Great-Gran's stories?"

"No, this isn't a story – it's real!" Olga stamped her foot with frustration at not being able to tell Sam about the oggies. "It is magic – and it keeps happening to me!"

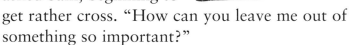

"Why can't you tell me, then?" asked Sam, beginning to get rather cross. "How can you leave me out of something so important?"

"They told me not to!" said Olga sadly. "There was a warning on the packet. They said something awful would happen to me if I told – and the magic would stop!"

"Warning on the packet?" said Sam in a puzzled voice. "Is it fireworks? Just tell me exactly what it said. That wouldn't be telling the secret, would it? Perhaps we can work something out if we think about it together. That's always worked for us before, hasn't it?"

Olga nodded. She could remember the exact

words on the greasy brown paper.

"It was a rhyme. It said, 'Beware all who trespass on my domain, don't seek to profit from unlawful gain'. That must mean that you can't use the oggies for anything bad – like stealing, I suppose. 'Wondrous oggies have the power all men desire, abuse that power, and your fate will be dire. If to any man the secret of the mine you tell, you will surely break the power of the oggies' spell'. That's why I can't tell you about it. 'But if you keep the secret, ever hold it true, every week an oggie will appear for you'. I do so want another oggie, Sam, that's why I can't tell you!"

"*Oggies!*" spluttered Sam. "Tiddy oggies like your mum makes for picnics and you always swap half for my yam fritters?"

Olga nodded silently.

"That's incredible! That's amazing! That's … that's not *magic*, that's food!" said Sam.

"Don't shout!" said Olga. "It's meant to be a secret, remember!"

"Tell me the rhyme again," asked Sam, "the bit after the dire warning."

Olga repeated the rhyme. "If to any man the secret of the mine you do tell …"

"Stop!" commanded Sam. "That's it! That's the loophole!"

"It's not a loophole, it's a rhyme," said Olga confused. "What are you *on* about, Sam?"

"A loophole is something you can use to your advantage," said Sam eagerly. "Something you can slip through to get out of a problem. Look at me, Olga!"

Olga looked at Sam. He looked much as he always looked – cheeky grin, curly black hair, skin glowing brown as a conker, big eyes that Olga always said should belong to a cow. She shrugged her shoulders and gazed at him with a look of bafflement. Sam put his fists on his hips, blew out his thin chest and put on a deep voice.

"How much of a man do I look like to you?" he growled, then gave her a mischievous grin.

Suddenly Olga jumped up and down with delight. **"If to any man the secret you do tell!"** she repeated. "You're not a man, Sam, you're a lit ..."

Sam gave her a warning look. He didn't like it mentioned that he, like Olga, was one of the smallest in top juniors.

"You're just a boy!" she said triumphantly. "You're a boy, not a man, so I can tell you the secret!"

"Exactly! Now tell me what happened and why you think oggies suddenly have magic powers!" said Sam eagerly.

"Come down to my back garden!" shouted Olga, and raced off down the road towards home.

Ten minutes later she had told him everything – all about the tunnel and the mine, then finding the hot oggie surrounded by years of dust. When she told him what she'd done to nasty Uncle Billy, Sam rolled over in the grass and howled with delight.

"This is so cool!" he kept saying. "We're going to have such fun with this! Did it say when you're going to get the next oggie?"

Olga shook her head. "No, but it did say every week, so I should get one next Saturday."

For the rest of the week Olga and Sam spent every spare moment searching for the hole to the tunnel or planning what to do with the next oggie. Olga was very relieved that Sam believed her so absolutely and was thankful for his great-granny

and her stories. He'd heard stories of magic since the day he was born, and Sam had always longed to get his hands on some of his own.

"What if we never find the hole again?" panted Olga, crawling out from under a bush and trying to brush the leaves out of her long red hair. "What's the good of a magic oggie if we can't even find it?"

They spent all day Saturday and Sunday in Olga's garden, looking for the oggie.

"Keep out of my raspberry bushes – the fruit's just ripening!" said Olga's dad, as Sam passed him on hands and knees. Sam had a large magnifying glass in his hand and was peering through it, as if the oggie might suddenly have become microscopic in size.

Mum was busy changing the oil in the motorbike she rode to work.

"For heaven's sake, Olga, why do you always look as if you've been dragged

through a hedge backwards?"
Mum asked, as Olga followed
Sam, peering down at every inch
of the ground, as if she'd lost a
pound coin. Olga looked up for a
moment.

"Probably because I have,"
she said thoughtfully, and
returned to her search.

"It's just a game,"
said her father from
his deckchair,

where he was enjoying the late autumn sun. "I know, it's a treasure hunt, isn't it?"

"Sort of," said Olga and crawled off under a bush.

Her parents looked at each other and sighed. "At least it keeps them quiet," said Mum thankfully.

"Maybe we can't find it because I told you the secret," said Olga miserably beginning to wish she hadn't. They were sitting in the jungle, their backs against the mossy old tree. "What will I do if we never find it again?"

"Never mind worrying about that," said Sam. "Let's think what we will do with a magic time-stopping oggie if we *do* get one? How far around you does time stop? Is it everywhere in the world, or just in Plymouth? Or is it just where you are?"

"I think it's just round where I am when I first start eating the oggie," said Olga thoughtfully, "but it stretches quite far away, too. The morris men stopped dancing and their drummer stopped beating his drum. But in the distance I could still hear things happening and people shouting."

"Wow!" said Sam longingly. "I can't wait! We could do anything – like paint the school purple, or use the photocopier to give everyone a letter announcing an extra day's holiday!"

"I know what I would do," said Olga. "Last week Miss Harper said that all dogs are truly horrible creatures – just because Rosie's new puppy peed on her shoe in the playground when she was talking to Rosie's mum about nits. I thought that was a mean thing for Miss Harper to do, because anyone could have heard and been nasty to Rosie."

"And the dog couldn't help it because he's just a tiny puppy and Miss Harper had been nagging away for ages," put in Sam.

"I'd put Miss Harper in the music room –

because it's soundproof," said Olga. "Then I'd make time stand still and fill the room up with the biggest, noisiest dogs I could find. Not nasty ones that would bite, but nice, sloppy, *licky* ones who would want to kiss her and slobber all over her!"

"Cool!" said Sam. "Where would you get the dogs from?"

"Hmmm," said Olga, who hadn't thought of that. "Well, are you going to help me look for this oggie, or not?"

5 Cookery Class

Olga had almost given up finding the promised oggie. Perhaps she *had* fallen asleep like Alice and dreamed the whole thing. Now it was Monday morning again, and nearly time to leave for school. Then she remembered. It was Purple Group's turn to do cookery. Olga loved cookery. She loved to make anything, but the things you could eat at the end were much the best.

"Mum, I need 50p cookery money to take to school today!" Olga yelled from the open back door.

Behind the door, about thirty centimetres from Olga's yell, Mum put her hands over her ears and groaned.

Olga looked out over the back garden, watching next door's cat creeping stealthily along the garden wall, trying to surprise a bird twittering in the apple tree.

"Get rid of that awful moggy, will you, Olga?" said Dad. He waged a constant war against the local cats, who all used his garden as their toilet and his plants and trees as their scratching posts. Olga obligingly ran out, waving her arms and shrieking. Dad always said that she was really good at scaring off the cats. Mum groaned again and absent-mindedly put her mug of hot coffee into the fridge. She wasn't at her best first thing in the morning.

Olga climbed up the apple tree, determined to make sure that the cat had gone. And there, in the crook of the old tree was an oggie! It was nicely browned, felt warm and smelled absolutely delicious.

She ran back up the path to the house, eager to tell Sam. She put the oggie safely inside her lunch box. Almost bursting with excitement, she raced through the house and out of the front door, yelling

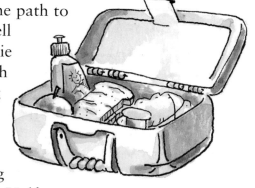

goodbye as she went. Half-way to school she realised she'd forgotten her homework, and had to go back for it. All that cat chasing made her late. Now she wouldn't be able to tell Sam about the oggie before school. *And* she had forgotten her cookery money. Miss Eagle would *not* be pleased.

Olga ran up to school in record time, only to see the lunch monitors pick up and carry off her lunch box as she hung up her coat. The morning had never passed so slowly. Sam raised his eyebrows questioningly at her, and she nodded her head hard. Neither of them could concentrate. The weekly spelling test was a disaster. Maths was even worse.

Cookery time came at last. "Purple Group to the resources room, quietly now," said Miss Eagle. Purple Group filed quietly down the corridor.

Miss Eagle was quite capable of calling them back to do extra spelling if they messed about.

Olga lagged behind the others as they headed towards the resources room. She stopped outside the dinner hall, where the plastic crates of lunch boxes were stored. Luckily, she found hers quite quickly and opened it. The oggie was still there.

"Olga!" came the squeaky voice of Mrs Harper, the classroom assistant. "Come into the resources room *immediately!*"

Olga put the oggie in her pocket and followed the others in.

"Please Miss, can I break the eggs?" she asked.

"Certainly not! A careless little girl like you would be sure to get eggshell in the bowl," Mrs Harper replied.

Olga felt most insulted. She'd been making cakes by herself for years at home, and felt herself to be an expert. Cracking eggs was her speciality. "But please, Mrs Harper, I'm really good at it!" Olga insisted.

"Don't go on about it, Olga. When I say 'No', I *mean* 'No'! I shall crack the eggs myself. You will watch carefully to see how it's done. Mr Reilly will be calling into the classroom later to sample our cakes and hear our new autumn poem. We want our headteacher to have something decent to eat, don't we, Purple Group?"

Purple Group glowered at Mrs Harper. It was obviously going to be one of those sessions when she did all the cooking, and the group did the watching – and the washing-up.

Mrs Harper bent over to check the height of the shelves in the oven. Fairy cakes had to be put on the top shelf. Olga broke off a big chunk of oggie and handed it to Sam.

"Just watch this!" she hissed. "Now!"

Both of them popped the pasty into their mouths at exactly the same time. As he sucked on the delicious lump of pastry Sam looked around him in amazement. Everything Olga had said was true!

Nobody was moving. Mrs Harper and Purple Group were all frozen into the positions they were in when they had popped in the oggie. Mrs Harper's large, flower-sprinkled bottom was still bent over by the oven door. Olga resisted a strong urge to put her foot on that flowery bottom and thrust her inside the oven, slamming the door on her forever, like the witch in Hansel and Gretel.

Behind Mrs Harper's back, Ben had been swinging, a hand flat on the table on each side of him. Now he was suspended in mid air, like an Olympic gymnast, his feet stretched out in front of him.

Kate's hand, holding a paper cake case, was poised above the cake tin. Henry's finger was stuck as far up his nose as it was possible to get, pushing his face out of shape like a comic book alien. Olga decided never to sample any of *his* cooking.

Alex was picking up a set of dropped measuring spoons. He was stuck under the table with only his feet sticking out. Tracey sat drooped over the table, her elbows holding her up. Her mouth was plugged completely with her thumb, and her eyes were closed. She was obviously just about to drop off to sleep. Perhaps she was telling the truth about always staying up to watch the late-night horror film. Walter, who sat next to her in class, was just standing there, like a surprised statue.

"This is so cool!" said Sam, his face one enormous grin. "This really happens *every* time a tiddy oggie is eaten? I was worried in case it would only happen once!"

Olga looked around at all the people the oggie had put into a trance.

"What shall we do?" she asked Sam.

A dozen wicked schemes flickered through her mind and departed.

"Think of something quick!" said Sam. "I haven't got much oggie left!"

Quickly she passed him another bit.

"Just watch this!" she muttered through her mouthful.

She filled a pan with hot water from the tap, turned on the stove and put all the eggs from the fridge into the pan.

A few minutes later, the hard-boiled eggs had been cooled under the cold tap and put back into the egg box. As they swallowed their last pieces of oggie, they took their seats opposite the mixing bowl at the table.

They wanted to be in the best position to enjoy watching Mrs Harper's face when she cracked those eggs.

"Now class, gather round and watch me," twittered Mrs Harper, as she came over to the table. "That means you too, Tracey! Wake up and pay attention, child! Sit *down*, Ben! I don't want to see you swinging on the desks again. Where are Olga and Sam? Oh, you're there, *and* paying attention for once, I see!"

Olga beamed at her happily. "Of course I'm paying attention, Miss!" she said politely. "I just *love* to watch you teaching me to cook. I'm sure I'll learn such a lot! Shall I pass you an egg?"

She picked up one of the eggs and reached over to hand it to Mrs Harper. Mrs Harper looked horrified at the sight of Olga handling the egg.

Next to her, Sam was already shaking with silent laughter, but Mrs Harper's eyes were fixed on Olga. The slight nudge of Sam's laughter was all Olga needed to toss the egg she was holding up into the air. She reached up to catch it again, fumbled, and the egg shot across the table.

Mrs Harper was gibbering wildly.

"Aarrggh! No! Stop! Dearie me! Olga! No! Aaarrrgggh!"

Sam shot out a thin arm and neatly caught the egg. He handed it carefully to Mrs Harper, who clutched it to her large chest.

"Oh, my heavens! Oh, my goodness! Oh, my

heart! Dearie me! Olga, don't you dare touch those eggs again, you naughty girl! Sit on your hands this minute!"

Olga obediently put both of her hands underneath her and sat on them, still beaming happily at Mrs Harper. The other children gathered round closely. They weren't sure what was going on here, but it was certainly more interesting than Mrs Harper's usual lesson.

"Now, watch carefully, Purple Group," said Mrs Harper. "There is only one correct way of breaking an egg. Hold it with both hands and tap it carefully on the side of the bowl, like this."

The egg made a dull thud as she tapped it on the bowl. A perplexed look came over Mrs Harper's face.

"Perhaps a *little* harder, then," she said. "You have to be ready to separate both halves of the egg immediately and let the raw insides fall into the bowl."

She tapped again and, hearing a successful crack, pulled the eggshell apart. Her mouth opened wide as a hard-boiled egg plopped into the bowl. The children giggled, all except Olga, who sat with her hands safely underneath her, an attentive look on her freckled face.

"You must have forgotten you'd cooked that

one already," she said sympathetically. "Try another one." Sam turned and winked at Olga.

Mrs Harper slowly reached out a hand for another egg, never taking her eyes off Olga's face. She cracked it on the side of the bowl. The second egg bounced into the mixing bowl. The children laughed aloud. Slowly, one after another, Mrs Harper cracked the eggs into the bowl. Soon six fat, white eggs nestled on the bottom of the bowl.

"How are we going to make fairy cakes with those, Miss?" asked Sam.

"How did you do that?" said Mrs Harper to Olga, in a low voice. "I bought those eggs only this morning. They were raw when I brought them in!"

"Me, Miss?" asked Olga innocently. "How did I do what? I've been sitting on my hands like you told me to!"

"I … you … aaarrrggghhh! I think I'm going to have to go and sit down in the staff room!" said Mrs Harper, going a strange shade of green and patting her chest.

When Mr Reilly visited their classroom later that day, Olga and Sam offered him some delicious egg sandwiches.

6 Carrots

Olga's godfather, Uncle Peter, had been to stay. He was short and bald, and said the same silly things every time he came to stay, which was once a year. He told the same jokes, too. They had been awful the first time Olga could remember hearing them, when she was about four.

But Uncle Peter always pressed a two-pound coin into each of Olga's eager hands when he left. Olga was allowed to spend Uncle Peter's money on absolutely anything she wanted – as long as it wasn't sweets. She hung over the garden wall, waving wildly as he drove away, a two-pound coin clutched tightly in each hand. Mum went indoors to get ready for work. Olga tried to jump down off the wall without using her hands. She lost her balance, and fell straight into the flower bed.

She soon forgot her horror at the vast array of squashed flowers when she saw another oggie nestled amongst the pansies. Mum heard the yell of delight from the house, but put it down to Olga's pleasure in suddenly becoming rich, and the relief at Uncle Peter's departure.

A week had passed since Olga had found her last oggie. But now, here was another one. Olga ran indoors, just managing to get the oggie into her bag before Mum came out, ready to see her off to school.

She ran happily up the road to school, jingling her money in her pocket. She couldn't wait to tell Sam about the oggie, and she had money to spend. What a wonderful day it was going to be! For once she was early for school. But Sam had not yet arrived. He came by bus, and often got there just as the bell was ringing.

Olga was sitting on a bench in the playground when three girls approached. Lisa was a tall, stringy girl

with enormous ears. Zoe was smaller, and quite
timid, except when Lisa was around. Gemma
lived in the same road as Olga. She
tended to push the little kids about,
although in the holidays she often
used to hang wistfully over
Olga's garden gate.
Olga's mum had even
been known to ask
her in to play, much
to Olga's horror.
The three girls
always
teased
Olga.

"Lost your boyfriend then, Carrots?" said Lisa spitefully.

"He's *not* my boyfriend! And don't you *dare* call me 'Carrots' again!" said Olga furiously.

"Oh look, she's going so red, you can't even see those millions and trillions of freckles," mocked Zoe.

"Do you know what freckles are, Carrots?" asked Gemma. "My mum told me. You get a horrid little freckly spot every single time you tell a lie. Did you know that? Now we all know that you've told absolutely masses of lies."

"That's rubbish!" Olga shouted back. "My mum says that freckles are the Sun's kisses – and she knows a lot more than your mother! So there!"

The three tormentors roared with laughter.

"Are you Mummy's sweet little sun-kissed babykins then, Carrots?" asked Lisa.

Before Olga could think of anything to say, Miss Eagle appeared in the playground and rang the bell. As they got into their lines, Gemma put out her foot and deliberately tripped Olga up.

"Let me tell you something," hissed Olga, as she got up. "If you don't leave me alone, and if you ever call me 'Carrots' again, something really terrible will happen to you. You won't know how or why, or what worse thing will happen next!"

"Oh, I'm so frightened!" laughed Lisa. "Little Carrots just scares me to death!"

The three girls ran on into school, rolling about with laughter at their own jokes.

Olga sat fuming through assembly. She couldn't help being small for her age, or having flaming red hair and loads of freckles. Above all, Olga hated, just hated, being called 'Carrots'. She had always been told to take no notice of name-calling. But that was one name she couldn't ignore. It always made her turn bright red with rage.

All morning Olga noticed the three girls constantly glancing at her and chatting together when Miss Eagle was looking the other way. They were obviously plotting something, and she was quite sure it was something to do with her. When first Lisa, and then Zoe and Gemma, asked to go to the toilet, she was sure of it.

Well, Olga wasn't going to stand for that, she'd sort them out. Stealthily, with her eyes on Miss Eagle, Olga reached into her bag and slipped the oggie into her pocket. Then she raised her hand and asked if she could be excused.

"Can't you wait until the others get back?" demanded Miss Eagle.

"No, Miss. I'm absolutely desperate," said Olga. Well, it was quite true really. She *was* desperate – to get her hands on those girls.

Sam waved his hand wildly. "Miss, I need to go, too."

"Olga, you can go if you must, but be quick," said Miss Eagle wearily. "Tell the other three to hurry back *now*. Sam, you can go when the girls get back."

Sam looked really disappointed as Olga left the classroom. Just as she had thought, those awful

girls were in the cloakroom. Gemma was busy
stuffing Olga's coat down behind the radiator.
Lisa and Zoe, giggling wildly, were throwing her
PE kit up onto the light fittings. Olga's trainers
were already in the sink, full of water, with a
congealing bar of soap sticking out of each one.
The wellies she'd left at school on the last rainy
day had been filled with sand and wedged behind
the lost property bin.

Olga felt like exploding. Then she had a brainwave. Something Mr Reilly had said in assembly came into her mind. "I believe in making the punishment fit the crime."

On that occasion he had made a guilty crisp-packet-dropper pick up all the litter in the playground every playtime for a week. Olga had an even better idea.

Quickly she popped a bit of oggie into her mouth. Instantly, time stood still in the cloakroom of Sir Walter Raleigh Primary School. Gemma remained with her arms squashed behind the radiator. Zoe and Lisa, hands high above their heads, looked like they were in a netball match.

Quick as a flash, Olga was out of the school door and across the playground. She slipped through the big school gates and into the street. She crossed the road at the pelican crossing and reached the greengrocer's shop in less than a minute. She was very glad to find it empty, except for the shop assistant. It seemed that time only stood still in the area around Olga when she took her first bite of oggie. She didn't know how well the spell would work when she wasn't there. Olga was very grateful to Uncle Peter for the money as she watched the shop assistant fill bag after bag with vegetables.

"Is this for a project you're doing in school then, lovey?" asked the shop assistant, curiously.

"Umm ... sort of ..." muttered Olga, through her mouthful of oggie.

She grabbed the bags and was back in school and into the cloakroom in no time. Nobody else had come into the cloakroom and the three girls were just as she had left them. She felt happy again as she arranged her shopping carefully. She swallowed her last bit of oggie as she dashed in through the classroom door.

"Miss Eagle, come quickly! Something's happened in the cloakroom! Something's happened to Lisa and Zoe and Gemma!"

Telling the class to get on with their work, Miss Eagle quickly followed Olga to the cloakroom. The three girls, looking very bewildered, were just as Olga had left them, seconds before.

There were carrots poking out of their sleeves, out of the necks of their shirts, from behind their ears. Carrots in their waistbands, carrots down their socks, carrots tied to their shoelaces. Lovely, long, orange carrots, all with bright green, springy tops that waved energetically about as the girls shook their heads in amazement.

There were carrots under their hairbands, carrots sticking out of their pockets, carrots everywhere. Gemma had carrots tied to the ends of her plaits. Lisa even had them dangling from her huge ears, like very strange ear-rings.

"Well girls, you've certainly got a lot of explaining to do!" said Miss Eagle at last, as she marched them off to Mr Reilly's office.

Olga had school dinners that day, as she'd forgotten her lunch box again. The carrots were delicious.

7 Science is a Slippery Subject

Olga hopscotched happily home from school at lunchtime one Friday, looking forward to a blissful afternoon. She thought of her class, cooped up with Miss Eagle, with only a science test to look forward to. Olga was going to the dentist. Not that she was a bit bothered about that.

She was only allowed sweets on Saturdays. Also, her mother made sure that she had the cleanest teeth in the school. When Mum was really mad with Olga, she tended to say, "Oh Olga! Go and clean your teeth!" Olga's teeth were perfect.

Dad would be taking her to the dentist. He had Friday afternoons off when he was going to be working on Saturday morning, and he always cooked a good, hot dinner, so Olga wouldn't even have to have boring old sandwiches and crisps. After the dentist she could help her dad in the garden. Maybe he'd let her help build a bonfire.

The afternoon stretched ahead in joyful freedom. Dad had just finished peeling the vegetables for dinner when Olga came into the kitchen.

"Hello, Olga," he said. "Dinner won't be long. Could you please take these down to the compost heap for me?"

He handed Olga a colander heaped with potato and carrot peelings and sprout leaves. Olga was glad to help; she loved to be in the garden. She went down to the compost heap beside the shed. She was just about to turn over the colander onto the green, fragrant heap when she saw it. Her weekly oggie, sitting on top of the compost heap like the king of the castle!

She snatched it up. She felt like eating it right away this time, it smelled so good. She suddenly felt really starving. But before she could open her mouth, she heard her father calling her in for dinner. Quickly Olga stuffed the oggie into her pocket. She dumped the peelings onto the compost heap, colander and all, and ran indoors.

After a very fine dinner, Olga and her father set out for the dentist. She really liked Mrs Freeman. She was always kind and gentle. She never said silly things like "Haven't you grown!" like most grown-ups who hadn't seen you for six months. They didn't even have to wait, and the check-up was over in seconds. They set off immediately for home, and reached the crossing by the school just as the bell went. The trip to the dentist had passed even quicker than usual.

"That was good timing," said Dad. "I'll say goodbye here then. See you after school."

"Whatever do you mean, 'goodbye'?" asked Olga anxiously. "Aren't I coming home with you?"

"Of course not, Olga. We didn't have to wait at the dentist, as your mum says you often have to do. Quickly now, the bell's already gone."

"But Mum *always* lets me come home after the dentist!" wailed Olga.

"But that's only if it's the middle of the

afternoon. You've got two hours left! In you go!"

Olga knew there was no arguing with her father, so in she went. Tears pricked her eyes as she went into the cloakroom to hang up her coat. She had been really looking forward to gardening with Dad. She hoped he wouldn't make the bonfire without her. She was so cross that she slammed the classroom door as she went through it. Miss Eagle looked up and sighed.

"That's no way to come into a room, Olga. I think you'd better go out and do that again."

It took all of Olga's self-control to go out and come back in quietly. She wanted to slam the door so hard that the glass cracked into a million pieces. Miss Eagle looked at Olga.

Olga looked at Miss Eagle, and then at Miss Harper. If looks could kill they would both have been struck down on the spot.

"Come and sit down, Olga, and stop glowering!" said Miss Eagle. "It's time for our science test. Well class, you've done so well in science this term that I'm sure you'll know all the answers. So I've decided to make it into a special spelling test, as well. There are twenty questions and for each question you'll get one mark for getting the scientific fact right, and four marks for getting the word spelled correctly. How many marks could you get then, class?"

There were a few shouts of "a hundred, Miss!" from the smart alecs, amid the general groans.

"That's right. And I don't want to see anyone get less than sixty. You've had all week to revise. Now get your pencils out."

Olga gasped. This was terrible! What could she do? She hadn't bothered to revise for the science test at all, because of the dentist appointment. She enjoyed science, and she was good at it. She could probably get at least sixteen of the answers right anyway. But that would only be sixteen out of a hundred.

Spelling was Olga's worst subject. She needed to work for ages to get even twelve out of twenty on the weekly spelling test. And a *science* spelling test! There'd be words like 'chemical' and 'electricity', 'chlorophyll' and 'chrysalis'. How many 'p's were there in pupa, and did 'volcanoes' have an 'e' before the 's' or not?

She just couldn't bear it. She didn't even have time to consult Sam, and he was too far away across the table to pass him some oggie without all the other children noticing. Afterwards, they would all be sure to remember something as unusual as that – even Walter Smith, who was one sandwich short of a picnic. Olga put her hand into her pocket and shoved a huge chunk of oggie into her mouth.

She looked around. Across the table Sam was a slim, brown statue, with his ruler pulled back, about to flick a scrunched up bit of paper across the room. In the next seat sat Walter, his mouth wide open, as usual. All round, boys and girls were frozen in the act of getting out their pencils, or sharpening them or scratching their heads.

Miss Harper stood by the door, looking as if she'd like to leave quickly. Miss Eagle was facing the old blackboard, chalk in hand. She was just about to write the first question. Olga looked about her wildly. What could she do? Perhaps she could tear up the question paper and throw it out of the window. She looked at the desk. No papers. The questions were obviously in Miss Eagle's efficient brain. Olga racked *her* brains. Something must be done to stop Miss Eagle writing those questions.

Inspiration dawned. She shot out of the classroom door, nearly knocking over the frozen statue of Miss Harper in her haste. Olga sped off down the corridor to the sick room. Here, one of the other classroom assistants was suspended in the act of rubbing Vaseline into the very slightly grazed knee of a little girl.

Olga grabbed the pot of Vaseline and hurtled back to the classroom. Climbing onto Miss Eagle's desk, she proceeded to rub the entire pot of Vaseline onto the blackboard, covering it from the very top to the bottom edge. It was quite difficult squeezing in front of Miss Eagle, but Olga just managed it.

She thought the usually tatty board looked quite different, glossy, black and shining.

More slowly now, feeling very relieved, Olga took the empty pot back. Then she returned to the classroom and giggled at the sight of her friends still caught in their strange positions. She sat down and swallowed the last bit of oggie.

When Miss Eagle tried to write her science spelling test on the board, the chalk slipped and slithered all over the place.

"Whatever's wrong with this board?" asked Miss Eagle, crossly. "I'm sure it was fine before lunch!"

Sam looked at Olga and lifted his eyebrows questioningly. Olga grinned and nodded. Sam punched the air in silent jubilation and Olga breathed a sigh of relief that he hadn't been cross at being left out. Sam was a good friend. She hadn't really wanted to have an oggie action without him, but she'd had to do something before Miss Eagle started to write.

"This board was fine this morning!" repeated Miss Eagle. She stood back and looked at it suspiciously. "Although it *does* look different – shinier somehow! What do you think, Miss Harper?"

"Perhaps someone's interfered with it, Miss Eagle," suggested Miss Harper. "One of the children perhaps?"

Olga held her breath and sank down lower in her seat, pretending to be engrossed in writing her name very carefully on her piece of paper.

"Oh no, that's impossible!" said Miss

Eagle firmly. "I was in the classroom working out this science test while the children were having their dinner. I didn't leave until the recorder group came in here to practise and they stayed right until the bell went. No, it must just be something that happens to these old boards in the course of time."

She tried rubbing the board with a cloth, but even a new piece of chalk slid across the board without making a mark. Eventually she gave up in disgust and threw the greasy chalk into the bin.

"It's no good, and I've got to meet a parent now," she said, with a sigh. "You'll just have to find something else to do with them, Miss Harper."

The slippery blackboard could never ever be written on again, despite much scrubbing with boiling water by the caretaker. It was old and dented anyway, and Miss Eagle hated it. Mr Reilly had to order a new, smart whiteboard for her instead.

Miss Harper got them all to write about 'My Favourite Hobby'. Olga wrote about making bonfires.

8 Star Pupil

"Could you hang this washing out for me before school, Olga?" said Mum. "I really need to fix something on my motorbike before I leave."

Olga didn't mind hanging out the washing, so she picked up the laundry basket and headed for the back lawn. She found the oggie straight away. It was in the little plastic basket dangling from the washing line, the one the pegs were kept in.

"How did they know?" wondered Olga aloud. "How did they *know* it would be me and not Dad or Mum hanging out the washing this morning?"

Still thinking about this vexing question, Olga put the oggie into her skirt pocket and wandered back into the house. She grabbed her coat and lunch box, then rushed out of the door to school. She quite forgot she hadn't actually hung up the washing. Mum found the basket when she came home from work, dry on top, with a sodden pile underneath.

Olga spent the morning thinking about what she could do with her oggie. Miss Eagle told her off three times for daydreaming and eventually said, "Well Olga, I don't think you'll be joining the rest of Purple Group for your pottery session if you go on like this. Now just sit up and pay attention."

For the rest of the morning Olga was a model pupil and did get to do pottery after all. She made a plant pot for her dad's birthday. After lunch Sam had chess club, so they didn't have time to discuss what to do with the latest oggie. Coming out of the lunch hall she broke off a piece of oggie and quickly handed it to him.

"Don't you dare eat it until we've decided what to do!" she warned him.

The whole
class had
art in the
afternoon
and
afterwards
Sam and Olga
were close
together for
the first time,
washing the
brushes in the sink at
the back of the
classroom.

"What are we going
to do?" hissed Sam. "That bit of oggie is burning
a hole in my pocket, we've got to do *something*
with it! Besides, I'm hungry again. I can't promise
I won't forget and just eat it!"

"Don't you dare, Sam!" said Olga, horrified.
"Nothing's happened that we really *need* the oggie
for, and we can't just waste it!"

"Sam and Olga, surely you've finished those
brushes by now?" said Miss Eagle. "Stop
chattering and come and sit down."

"It's wasting it to do nothing!" Sam muttered,
slopping the last jar of paint water into the sink.

"And Walter Smith, do hurry up and finish cleaning out the hamsters," said Miss Eagle, in a sharper voice than she usually used towards Walter. "It's time for history."

Miss Eagle desperately wanted to encourage Walter, and was always giving him little jobs. But somehow Walter always managed to mess them up. He could forget things, spill things, break things and fall over things more easily than anyone Olga had ever met.

When he was born, his mother had wanted to give him 'Sir Walter Raleigh' for his first names. She thought plain old 'Smith' needed something posh to brighten it up, and what could be better than the name of the famous Elizabethan explorer. If it was good enough for the school they'd all been to, then it was good enough for her son.

His father had put his foot down about the 'Sir' bit. But his mother still insisted on calling him Walter Raleigh at home. The other kids laughed themselves silly whenever they heard, *'Walter Raleigh, come in for your tea!'* being roared down the street.

Miss Eagle tried to remember to call him that when his mother came on parents' night, but usually she just called him 'Walter'. Olga sympathised about his name. Sometimes it was difficult being called Olga.

Walter had already finished with the hamsters and had just started working on the wormery next to the sink. That was silly for a start, as worms are the one pet that really *don't* need cleaning out. Walter had picked up one of the worms and was dangling it in front of his eyes. Open-mouthed, he was peering at it very closely, as if trying to decide which one it was.

Olga flicked a handful of wet brushes into the sink, just as Sam bent over it to pick up one he'd dropped.

"Hey, be careful!" he yelped, as the water, still not very clean, spattered all over him.

He was beginning to get cross about the oggie. Why should Olga always decide what to do with it?

Olga was feeling just as annoyed. Why didn't Sam understand that you couldn't waste the power of an oggie on just anything? She pushed past him grumpily as she went to sit down at her table. Sam gave her a little shove back and Olga staggered into Walter.

She muttered, "Sorry!" rather crossly as she sat down. Immediately she heard a strange gulping noise from Walter and turned quickly. His fingers were empty, but his eyes nearly bulged out of his head.

"What's the matter, Walter?" asked Olga. "Did you drop the worm on the floor? Shall I help you find it?"

Walter pointed wordlessly to his mouth. He opened it, but no sound came out.

"Sit down, Sam, and you too, Olga and Walter," said Miss Eagle. "We must get *some* work done this afternoon." As they sat down Olga whispered, "What happened, Walter? Where's the worm?"

"I ate it!" groaned Walter. "I didn't mean to – it just sort of fell into my mouth and I automatically swallowed it! Please don't tell Miss Eagle, Olga!"

Olga felt really bad then. It wasn't Walter's fault that she and Sam were arguing. If she hadn't pushed past Sam and he hadn't pushed her it would never have happened – probably. But you never knew with Walter. Things like that just seemed to happen to him. She peered at his face. Was he already beginning to look a bit green? She liked Walter and hadn't meant to make him swallow that worm. What could she do to make it up to him?

Suddenly the class Star Chart caught her eye.
Every week Miss Eagle put up a new Star Chart.
She felt it helped to encourage those children who
might not be particularly clever, but who tried hard.
You could get a star for good work, or
for being especially
helpful or well-
mannered. The
person with the most
stars got a prize on
Friday afternoon. The
prizes were small – a
sheet of stickers, a
notebook or a novelty
pencil sharpener – but
Miss Eagle's class always
tried hard for the award.

But this week the Star
Chart looked rather bare.
It was getting near to the end of term and the
children were restless and overexcited. It had been
really windy all week and for some reason that
always played havoc with the children's behaviour.
Although Olga had won the prize before, she
knew she had no chance of it this week. It was
usually won with five or six stars and she had
only one.

In fact, the highest number of stars this week was only three. Walter had two stars. This in itself was pretty amazing. It was the first time he had ever got more than one in a week. Miss Eagle did try to award him stars, but Walter was a natural disaster area. Poor Walter. Looking at the chart, Olga felt even more guilty about the worm.

Olga caught Sam's eye across the table and nodded vigorously. She took her oggie from her pocket and saw Sam grin and do the same. She nodded again and they both took a mouthful at the same time. Everyone in the classroom froze.

"What's going on?" asked Sam eagerly.

"When I pushed you and you pushed me, we managed to shove Walter and he swallowed that worm he was dangling!" said Olga, as she went over to Miss Eagle's desk.

"Walter *ate* the worm! What a wal ..." began Sam, then noticed the look on Olga's face and said, "What a shame! Ugghh! What are we going to do?"

"We're going to make it up to him," said Olga.

She borrowed Miss Eagle's glue stick from the desk. Then she carefully peeled off the star after her own name and one of Sam's two stars. She added them to the two stars on the line that said 'W. R. Smith'. She would never have dreamed of adding stars to her own name, but she felt that for Walter it was justified. Putting the glue back on the desk she and Sam sat down again and swallowed their last bit of oggie.

They had history for their last lesson and, despite herself, Olga really enjoyed it. Miss Eagle was a good teacher and could make history really come alive. Then it was time for Miss Eagle to award the Star Chart prize. Checking the chart, she saw that Walter had four stars. She didn't remember giving him that many stars but perhaps Miss Harper had also given him some. Miss Harper did cookery with another class last thing on Friday afternoons, so Miss Eagle couldn't ask her.

"I'm very happy to award this week's 'Star

Pupil' prize to Walter Smith."

The class was as surprised as she was, but it was late on Friday afternoon and they were all in a good mood now. Cheers rang out and Sam waved his arms and stamped his feet. Walter just sat there with his mouth open as usual. Then, as he realised what had happened, a huge grin spread slowly across his face. Olga thought he looked like the picture of the Cheshire cat in *Alice in Wonderland*.

Miss Eagle called everyone to attention. "Quieten down, everyone!" she said. "It's nearly time to go home, so we might as well all calm down with a bit of *Alice in Wonderland*." She began reading. "'Off with their heads!' said the Duchess!"

Sam and Olga sat back and exchanged happy grins. It hadn't been a good day for the worm, but at least Walter was pleased.

9 Pixies and Rodents

It was getting near to the end of term. Christmas was coming. Olga was getting pretty fed up with school. She wanted the term to be over. She wanted to be at home, making decorations and presents. She wanted to pop popcorn, and thread it onto long, red strings to hang on the tree. She wanted it to snow.

"Never mind," said Mum encouragingly, "it's not long to go now. Tonight we'll make chocolate decorations. Why don't you go out and play on the swing for a while before school. We won't have weather as mild as this for much longer."

That cheered Olga up a bit. Swinging always calmed her down and she was looking forward to the chocolate making. It was fun breaking up the big bars of chocolate to be melted down in the double boiler. Then pouring the melted chocolate carefully into the Christmas moulds. She loved the way the chocolate snapped so easily out of the mould when it was set. It was so easy to do but it looked so perfect. Santas, snowmen, stockings, bells and stars would be wrapped up in coloured foil and hung on the tree. It was such a good feeling to hand a chocolate Santa over to a friend and say, "I made it myself."

She swung back and forth, back and forth on the swing, happily daydreaming, until her mother called her in for school.

Jumping down from the swing, she nearly squashed it. It was there, right under the swing, her oggie. It couldn't have been there when she got on the swing, she'd have seen it. Who had put it there, and when and how?

Still, there it was. Happily tucking it into her pocket, Olga went to school in a better frame of mind. It didn't last. She had forgotten – it was 'Happy, Helpful Pixie Day'.

Years and years ago, in the Dark Ages, there had been a little girl at Sir Walter Raleigh Primary School called Pixie Sprott. Olga thought it was unfortunate enough to be called Pixie Sprott, without telling the world about it. Even worse, Pixie Sprott was now Mrs Pixie Rumplebottom.

According to herself, Mrs Rumplebottom had been the happiest, most helpful little pixie any teacher could have the good fortune to meet. Pixie just loved to lend a helping hand to everyone she came across. She had married a very rich carpet manufacturer called Buzz Rumplebottom. As she constantly told everyone, "Pixie just loves to *buzz* about and share her happiness with others."

One of the ways Mrs Rumplebottom did this was to give a yearly present to her old school. This was usually something substantial like a television or a new computer. To get this useful gift, Mr Reilly agreed to have a 'Happy, Helpful Pixie Day' every year. He would have preferred not to have it so near to the end of the Christmas term though. But Mrs Rumplebottom thought it was the perfect way to get everyone filled with the Christmas spirit.

The whole school had to gather to listen to Mrs Rumplebottom's ghastly do-gooding stories. Every year they were exactly the same. Olga could recite them word for word, and sometimes did, to amuse her friends. But Olga pretended to be sick between sentences. Then Mrs Rumplebottom presented some child with the 'Happy, Helpful Pixie Award'. This was not quite as bad as it sounded, for as well as getting their names engraved on the trophy, the prize-winning little pixie got a book token. This was presented by Pixie herself, on stage, in front of the whole school.

Although generally happy and more often than not helpful, Olga was unlikely to be chosen for this award. It required some other quality that was never named, but easily identified – a smarmy, stuck-up, goody-goody attitude!

Anyway, along with just

about every one in the school, Olga couldn't think of anything more embarrassing than winning the 'Happy, Helpful Pixie Award', in spite of the book token.

"I don't think I'm going to be able to live through this *again*," groaned Sam miserably, as they sat down on the floor of the school hall.

"I think we could liven it up just a little this time," whispered Olga with a grin, patting the bump in her skirt pocket.

"Is it …?" asked Sam, forgetting to whisper in his excitement.

"Who's talking down there?" said Miss Eagle sternly.

Sam and Olga both sat up and folded their arms, looking the picture of innocence. Miss Eagle kept her eagle eye on both of them for some time. She was quite capable of separating them before Olga had a chance to pass a bit of oggie to Sam, so they both looked straight ahead, as if they were dying to find out how to be happy, helpful little pixies.

They watched Mrs Rumplebottom on the stage, waving her plump hands with their many rings, as she told her stories. At one point her hand caught the edge of her glass of water and sent it flying into Mr Reilly's lap.

"What the …?" he shouted, at the top of his

voice. Mr Reilly leaped up and down, trying to shake the water from his trousers and frowning at the Year Ones who were giggling in the front.

"Don't worry, Mrs Rumplebottom," he said through gritted teeth. "No damage done. Accidents *will* happen."

After the fuss had died down, Mr Reilly sat there, looking like a new infant who had just wet his pants.

Watching the tiny hat perched precariously on Mrs Rumplebottom's enormous bouffant hairdo, Olga was reminded of a nest. A little nest sitting on the top of a haystack. A little *empty* nest.

Still gazing attentively at Mrs Rumplebottom, Olga carefully eased the oggie from her pocket, broke off a big chunk and passed it to Sam.

As soon as she was sure that Miss Eagle was looking the other way she dug Sam in the ribs with her elbow. Simultaneously they both ducked their heads and took a secret bite of oggie. The whole school froze. Sam leaped to his feet and just stood there, looking at the school of statues, a huge grin on his face.

Mrs Rumplebottom had been waving both hands in the air to illustrate a point, so she remained stuck in that position. The teachers' last expressions were also firmly frozen to their faces.

"Just look at all the teachers!" laughed Sam. "They look as bored as we are! They look like the queue at the supermarket! What shall we do to liven things up, Olga?"

Sam had never had all the teachers at his mercy before – it was a dream come true! "I know, let's give them all a short haircut! We could sweep up all the hair – and they'd never know how it happened!"

"We'd never get in done in time," said Olga. "Besides, Miss Eagle has nice hair!"

"We could dress Mrs Rumplebottom up in one of the elf costumes from the Christmas play!" said Sam, so excitedly that his bit of oggie nearly fell out of his mouth. "They have pixie hoods and everything! Don't you think that would be a good idea?"

"No!" said Olga firmly. "Come with me, Sam!"

Olga carefully crept over the crossed legs of her classmates and went back into her classroom. Through her mouthful of oggie she explained to Sam exactly what they were going to do. Sam hooted with laughter and ran to get a cardboard box. Olga carefully put in it what was needed.

They ran back to the hall with the cardboard box. Sam and Olga climbed up onto the stage where all the staff were sitting in rows on each side of Pixie Rumplebottom. Sam held the box while Olga reached up to the silly little straw hat.

She carefully placed the six classroom white mice into the nest on the top of the haystack. Then both children leaped down and rejoined their class on the floor. Swallowing their last bits of oggie,

Olga and Sam settled down to enjoy the fun.

It was a little while before any of the mice ventured out. But soon a little twitching nose and long whiskers appeared over the side of the nest. Then the mouse put its tiny paws on the rim of the hat and sniffed the air. The school tittered, then giggled, then roared with laughter.

Pixie beamed. She thought that her stories were really going down well with the little dears this year. The first mouse slid down the haystack and toppled off the edge. It tumbled straight into the glass of water that Mr Reilly had kindly refilled.

As the second deluge of ice water cascaded into his lap Mr Reilly decided that the school definitely had enough computers and televisions now.

The next two mice leaped out of the nest simultaneously, like two athletes responding to the starter's gun. Going in opposite directions, they ran along the two lines of teachers and classroom helpers. They jumped from head to shoulder to head, to the ends of the rows. They reached the ends of the rows together, leaped to the floor and disappeared in opposite directions, never to be seen again.

The next mouse somersaulted into Pixie's outstretched hands. It took one look at her

startled face, then ran along the table and from there took an enormous leap onto the piano. It ran along the keys, producing a perfect scale, before disappearing inside. It lived inside the piano happily throughout the Christmas holidays, and then it ambled back to its cage in the classroom.

Mouse number five jumped straight off the back of the haystack, under the table, off the stage and right into the middle of the assembled school. Children fled in all directions, yelling, laughing or screaming, according to their characters. Sam captured it and put it safely into his top pocket.

He recognised it as his favourite mouse, and took it home until after the holidays, to recover from its experiences.

The uproar had died down a bit by the time the last little mouse emerged. It leaped gracefully onto the table and ran along to the end, where Mrs Harper was sitting. Her elbow was resting on the table while she fanned her hot, red face with a rolled-up pile of papers. She saw the mouse. She froze in horror. The mouse ran along her arm and up to the end of the rolled-up papers.

Here it waited a second, poised as if on the end of a diving board. Then it dived straight through Mrs Harper's loose, open collar into the dark reaches of her ample bosom. She jumped to her feet and gave an ear-splitting shriek that echoed round the school. You could see the stretched fabric of her dress rippling as the mouse scurried about, looking for a way out. There was an enormous crash as she fell to the floor in a dead faint. The mouse escaped gratefully the way it had come and scrambled up the curtains. There had *never* been a 'Happy, Helpful Pixie Day' like this before.

Sam was rolling on the floor with laughter, like many of his classmates. Olga helpfully fetched Mrs Harper a glass of water, then sat down quietly, perfectly satisfied with the results of this week's oggie action.

She'd livened up the dreaded Pixie Day, tonight she was making chocolates and soon it would be Christmas. Even better, a big fall of snow was forecast for the holiday. Her cousins were coming from London to stay with her.

As soon as it snowed she'd take them to the park to play in the snow and challenge them to a snowman-making contest. She'd arrange to meet Sam there, with the buckets and big shovels his dad used on his allotment. They could eat a bite of oggie and roll a snowball down the big hill to make it huge. Then they'd spend a good long time with their shovels and buckets, making the biggest snowman that the world had ever seen. Olga couldn't wait to see their faces when they finished the oggie and her cousins turned around and saw the world's most gigantic snowman.